Alphabet Kids™ Created by Allegr

Isaac's Zoo

Based on a story by Allegra Joyce Kassin

Written by **Neme Alperstein** *and* **Patrice Samara**
Illustrated by **Carol Nicklaus** *and* **Susan Unger**

TOYCHEST™
interactive

Meet the Alphabet Kids: Allegra, Elena, Isaac, Oni, Umar, and Yang.

They call themselves the Alphabet Kids because that's where they like to hang out — at the Alphabet Afterschool Center.

One day, Isaac couldn't wait to arrive home. That morning, his mom and dad had left for vacation, and *Bubbe*, his grandma, had come to stay with him.

"*Bubbe!*" Isaac yelled, as he ran up the driveway.

"I have a surprise for you," *Bubbe* said.

"Goldfish!" Isaac shouted, when he saw his surprise swimming around in circles.

"Thank you, thank you, *Bubbe!*" said a very happy Isaac. "I've always wanted a pet, and now I have two!"

"Having a pet is a big responsibility," cautioned *Bubbe*.

"I'm sure I'll be able to take care of my goldfish, once I learn what to do," said Isaac.

"It's easy," said *Bubbe*. "Feed them twice a day with just enough flakes to eat right away. Change the water and clean the bowl once a week. Make sure the water is not too hot and not too cold."

"I will, *Bubbe*. I promise!" said Isaac.

Then Isaac went off to Elena's house to play. Elena was playing the piano. Her cat, Coco, was curled by her feet.

"Guess what?" Isaac said. "My *Bubbe* gave me two pet goldfish."

"Goldfish aren't real pets. You can't play with them," answered Elena, rubbing Coco between the ears.

Isaac wished he could rub his goldfish between the ears.

On his way home, Isaac saw Oni and Allegra in the playground.

"My *Bubbe* gave me two pet goldfish," he said proudly.

"Too bad goldfish can't play catch like my dog, Duffy," Allegra said.

"Too bad goldfish can't talk like my parrot, Polly!" said Oni.

"Too bad! Too bad!" Polly squawked.

Isaac wished his goldfish could talk.

"At least I have two pets," said Isaac. "Even if they don't talk."

Isaac turned around and noticed that Yang had arrived.

"I have a pet, too!" said Yang. "Missy, my mouse, squeaks all night long."

"I have to go home now," Isaac said sadly. Isaac wasn't feeling so excited about his pets any more.

That night, *Bubbe* cooked chicken soup with *matzoh* balls, Isaac's favorite. But Isaac didn't feel very hungry. He looked sadly at his goldfish.

"What's the matter?" asked *Bubbe*. "Don't you like your new pets?"

"All my friends have pets they can play with — a cat, a dog, a parrot, and a mouse," said Isaac.

"Sounds like quite a zoo," said *Bubbe*.

All of a sudden, Isaac shouted excitedly, "A zoo! Great idea, *Bubbe!* Can I invite my friends over to bring their pets here?" asked Isaac. "Can I, *Bubbe?* Pleeeease!"

"It will be a lot of work," answered *Bubbe.* "What would your mom and dad say?"

"I think they would let me," said Isaac, although he wasn't so sure.

"Okay. For you, I'll do it," said *Bubbe.*

"Thank you, thank you! It will be so much fun!" said Isaac excitedly. Now it was *Bubbe* who wasn't so sure.

The next day, after school, *Bubbe* helped Isaac make signs to get ready for the big day.

"Tomorrow is the big day," Isaac said to his goldfish. "We're having a zoo in our backyard. Isn't that great?"

His goldfish just looked back at him, blowing bubbles.

Isaac hoped they understood.

Isaac woke up early to a beautiful day.

After breakfast, *Bubbe* helped Isaac put two long tables in the backyard. Isaac put three bowls of water on the back porch.

"These are for the thirsty animals," he said.

"I'll make lemonade for the thirsty kids," said *Bubbe*.

Elena arrived carrying Coco.

"What's in your pocket?" asked Isaac.

"Coco's toy mouse," said Elena. "Hide it anywhere, and Coco can find it."

She handed Isaac a wiry brush. "Here's Coco's brush to keep his fur nice and smooth. Would you like to brush Coco?" Elena asked.

"I'll brush Coco," answered *Bubbe*. "I love cats, and I'll make sure Coco won't get too close to the goldfish, just in case."

"In case of what?" asked Isaac.

"Never mind," said *Bubbe*. "I'll take Coco's toy mouse and I'll bring Coco outside later."

The zoo was turning out to be a great party! Isaac and *Bubbe* could hear all sorts of suggestions.

"Tell my turtle jokes!"

"Give my hamster rides in your pocket!"

"Catch some bugs for my snake!"

"Give my toad a bath!"

"Sing to Missy the mouse."

Isaac's zoo was getting quite full. Suddenly a voice shouted, "Hello! Hello!" Polly the parrot sounded just like a person.

Everyone was having a great time—except for Isaac.

Isaac was worried. There were so many pets in the yard. Things were getting out of hand!

Just then the kids heard an ice cream truck.
"Ice cream!" they all shouted, and off they ran, leaving Isaac alone in the yard with all the pets.

Isaac looked around. To his surprise, he noticed that some of the cages had been left open. "Oh no!" he said aloud.

"Oh, no! Oh, no!" said Polly the parrot, imitating Isaac.

Isaac hurried to close the cages, running from one to another. The hamster was still in his cage. The toad was still in his jar, and the ants were still in the ant farm.

But where was Missy the mouse?

"Uh, oh," thought Isaac. "I'd better find Missy fast!"

"This is for you," said Yang, handing Isaac a cone.

"Gee, thanks," said Isaac. "Missy is not in her cage," he whispered. Isaac didn't want anyone else to hear. "Missy is missing."

"What? Missy's missing?" Yang burst into tears.

"I'm sorry," said Isaac. "Her cage was left open. She has to be here somewhere. I'll help you find her."

"OY!" *Bubbe* shrieked from the house. *Oy* was her favorite yell when she didn't like something that was happening.

Everyone ran into the house.

"It's a mouse, and it's under the sofa!" *Bubbe* shouted. And there was Coco, right on the sofa, waiting to pounce.

"Coco is going to catch Missy!" cried Elena. "No, Coco, no! It's Missy, Yang's mouse. Missy is not a toy!"

Bubbe had no intention of touching Missy.

"Got her!" shouted Isaac, catching Missy. Coco looked disappointed and came down off the sofa.

"Here she is," said Isaac, handing Missy to Yang.

"It's been a long day. It's time for all of you to take your pets home," said *Bubbe*. *Bubbe* was tired, and did not want any more pets to escape.

After everyone had left, Isaac said, "Pets are a lot of work, *Bubbe*."

"They sure are," said *Bubbe*. "Of all the pets, which was your favorite?"

"I'll show you," said Isaac. "I forgot to tell you I gave them names Meet Goldie and Sam," he said proudly.

That night, a tired Isaac climbed into bed after he gave *Bubbe* a kiss goodnight. He glanced at Goldie and Sam. They didn't bark or squeak or meow or say "Goodnight, Goodnight," like Polly the parrot.

They didn't do anything but silently swim around in circles.

"Goodnight, Goldie. Goodnight, Sam. You're not any trouble at all. I wouldn't trade you for all the pets in the world," said Isaac as he happily drifted off to sleep.